Introduction

This fictional story is dedicated to every young

woman or girl around the world who was

kidnapped due to Human Trafficking, and the

International Labor Organization reports that

there are 40.3 million cases of human trafficking

globally have taken place. My prayers are with

the families of these victims.

With this story, "the Search for Lydia," I wanted

to shine a beacon of light upon things like this

that occur almost daily in some parts of the

world. Texas, Florida, New York, and California

have some of the highest rates of human

trafficking, and globally, Pakistan, Indonesia,

China, India, and Bangladesh are in the top 10

for human trafficking cases.

Chapter 1

A Kidnapping Takes Place

 Detective Hopkins kept a bulletin board on his wall at

home showing pictures of all the missing persons within

the past year, but when he took a tact and posted

Lydia's picture, he grabbed his coffee and sat thinking

for about twenty to thirty minutes, for one he thought

this particular case was a bit strange knowing that she

was just adopted by a new set of parents and things

were going great. Then suddenly, she goes missing. The

night Steven and Lydia drove to the supermarket to pick

up a few things before her summer vacation with her aunt, Vivian was typically the norm for her, but as they entered the store, the two split up. Steven went to aisle twelve to look at a specific type of shampoo his wife told him to grab, and Lydia went to the restroom.

Steven became a bit concerned after her being there for quite some time, Steven went to stand outside the door of the ladies bathroom and called out Lydia's name, but he got no answer. He even sends one of the store's employees inside to check if she's there, but she's gone! So, he went to look around the store, and no sign of her anywhere; they had just missed each other. As Lydia came out of the restroom, she began looking for her dad, but there were two guys who both looked Hispanic. One was on his phone, but the other was snapping pictures of Lydia from afar. Lydia had no idea that her dad was still in the store, so she happened to walk to the car to see if he was there, not knowing that she was being watched; during this time, it had gotten late, so it was dark outside. The store didn't have much lighting outside. One of the guys that were watching Lydia quickly pulled his car around, and as she noticed the car, she saw nothing but bright headlights, which was a white cargo van, and the other guy ran up behind

Lydia and grabbed her, but Lydia bit him on the arm and then slapped her. They scuffle for about twenty seconds until he overpowers her and drags her inside the van as the sliding doors close behind her. The door closed and locked as they sped off with Lydia inside! By the time Steven looks all over the store, he goes to the parking lot and sees Lydia's blue scarf lying on the ground with small specs of blood on it. At this point, Steven is in a state of shock and has no explanation for his wife on what happened to their daughter. By the time he gets home, he breaks the news to his wife gently but nervously and says, "someone took Lydia." First, she's calm, "what do you mean someone took her." Why is

she not here with you? Again, Steven says, this time in a

bit of a rage, she's gone, Michelle! Michelle starts crying

and yells, "the only child we ever had is gone." The Two

didn't sleep the whole night. Michelle stayed up until

dawn, but Steven fell asleep for an hour just before 6:00

am arrived. As they showered and changed clothes,

neither one ate breakfast. They lost their appetite. They

both get in the car and drive down to the police station

to file a missing person's report and as they enter the

police station Detective Brown politely says, "how can I

help you?" As Steven holds his wife in his arms, he tells

the Detective, our daughter Lydia went missing last night, and we have no whereabouts as to where she could be. All I have is the blue scarf she dropped on the ground outside the store we both went to yesterday evening. Detective Brown offers the two a seat in a small room for questioning, so Brown specifically asks Steven. Did you happen to see anybody following you and your daughter while on the way to the supermarket? No, Steven says, I didn't pick up any suspicious activity about weird vehicles following us. Michelle, sitting there in a state of shock again, starts crying and screaming, please, please help us find our daughter! So, Detective Brown gathered all the evidence from questions he could get now and said ok, you two can go home and try to get some sleep, with the sole intent of trusting that my partner and I would do the best we could find Lydia, but he then says, I can't promise you anything. On the way home, Michelle smells her daughter's scarf. With that being the only thing left of her, Michelle looks over at Steven while he is driving and says, what if she's dead, Steven says don't think like that! Try to stay positive about us finding her, he says. Santa Fe was a small town of people who mostly stayed to themself. Almost two weeks passed by, and still no sign of Lydia anywhere. Detectives made posters with images of Lydia at intersections on light poles along with posters at local supermarkets that said missing person on the front of them. Luckily there were surveillance cameras outside the store the night Lydia was kidnapped. Detective Hopkins went to the store and asked the store manager if he and Detective Brown could look over the camera's tapes to see what happened that night. The cameras caught everything, but the two guys had masks on, so they couldn't quite identify who they were, but the store manager quickly said, "hold on, let's rewind to back when they were in the store," and sure enough, the two guys were

identified, the next day detectives ran a search on the

two guys, their record showed that one of the guys by

the name of Emmanuel Lopez did fifteen years for rape.

The other, whose name was Roberto Diaz, was under

close watch for human trafficking charges, but police

couldn't charge him without enough evidence.

Chapter 2

The Abandoned Warehouse

About 30 miles west of Santa Fe was an abandoned

warehouse that led to an underground area. This area

had about twenty rooms. There was a girl in every

room, along with one guy watching the door. One guy

was going from room to room, bringing each girl drugs,

which were heroin and pills. This underground area had

an exit way that was about a hundred feet to get to the

outside towards the back; about eighteen girls were

there. Half of them were teenagers, and the other half

were adult women being held beneath this warehouse.

The warehouse looked as if no one ever went there, and

no one who drove by would think that the warehouse

led to a place with twenty rooms underneath. It was a

Friday night, and all the girls were sitting outside their

rooms drugged up with their eyes rolling to the back of

their heads. Some were crying, and others were too

high to realize what was happening. They all looked

upstairs and heard screaming and footsteps coming. It

was the two guys who kidnapped Lydia the night at the

supermarket, they had a cloth over her head, and as

one of them removed it, Lydia spat in the guy's face.

They scuffle after they get her untied while taking her to the empty room all the way down close to the end of the hallway of the underground area. But while in the van earlier on, Lydia, with her quick thinking, screams to the top of her lungs, saying, "I can't breathe, I can't breathe." Little did they know that she was lying; and was just trying to get a glimpse of where they were taking her; she wanted to see some landmarks. They removed the cloth from over her head for about twenty seconds. She starts coughing while at the same looking in every direction outside the van, she sees a waffle house and a Walmart, and by this time, they begin to

cover her head back up.

Meanwhile, underground the two guys dragged Lydia to

her room as the girls outside their rooms watched,

crying in sorrow for Lydia because they knew what she

was about to go through. As they threw her in the

room, she quickly jumped into the bed, curled up in a

ball with her head towards her knees, screaming out of

frustration. The two detectives had flyers all over town,

and they were even going from door to door at homes

to ask residents to show them the poster asking if

they'd ever seen the ten-year-old Lydia within the past

week or two ago. They even printed pictures of the white cargo van from the store's video camera, but little did detectives know that was a homeless guy outside the store the night that Lydia was abducted. After the homeless guy saw everything, he ran to the nearest mom-and-pop store in that area to grab a pen and write down the license plate number of the van. He didn't go into the supermarket that night because he didn't want anything to do with what was going on. Well, at least he didn't want to be seen. But one day, the homeless guy saw a poster showing a picture of Lydia. The guy realized that it was the same girl from the night everything happened at the supermarket. So, he

decided to take the info of the license plate number to

the nearest police station, which was just downtown in

Sante Fe. Once this news got to the Detectives working

the case, they were all over it. Because when they

watched the tape at the supermarket that night, the

cameras didn't show an angle of the license plate. So,

with this, they knew they were on to something. Now all

they had to do was find out where this van was located,

but Detectives realized that they'd have to put out a

much broader search than just the region of Sante Fe if

they were going to find this van.

Chapter 3

<u>Left on The Porch</u>

Lydia spent a few years living in the foster home Long before Steven and Michelle (Foster Parents) chose to adopt her. When Lydia was an infant, her real mom was on drugs really bad. One day her mom couldn't take it anymore and decided to leave Lydia on a random person's doorstep with a note attached to her; the note read, "please watch over my daughter and get her in the safest hands as possible Because my life is a mess right now." A little boy came to the doorstep after he heard the doorbell ring and told his mom, Mom! "There

is a baby on the porch," a lady who happens to be a

stay-at-home mom saw Lydia, an innocent infant, in a

baby seat, just staring at the little boy and the mother

of the home. The mother immediately starts crying out

of concern, at this point not knowing what to do next.

She sits with the baby throughout the day, feeding and

rocking her to sleep. As soon as the father gets home,

they discuss what's going to take place with the child,

the father comes up with the idea to take the child to a

foster home, and Lydia has been in foster care ever

since. While in the foster home, Lydia gets a roommate

one afternoon. Her roommate's name is Lisa. Lisa was troubled the day she set foot in Lydia's room. As the two go out for recess, Lisa asks Lydia if she'd like to smoke a cigarette with her. Lydia couldn't turn down the peer pressure as she replied, "sure, why not? It couldn't hurt." Lydia had no idea who her birth parents were, and she didn't even know how she ended up at the foster home after so many years. Long before she was adopted, one day, she was rambling through some paperwork in an office at the foster care. She found out a few things about her mom; after that, she looked her up on the computer and wrote down some key factors that she needed to know. Lydia was tired of living at the

foster home. Some nights she would fold her hands and

ask God to help her find her birth parents one day or at

least her mom. Lydia liked to draw in her spare time,

but one day she asked one of the women working at the

foster home to buy her some paintbrushes and a canvas

to paint on. From that day on, she started painting

things she had seen with her eyes around her. She

became so good that they started entering her paintings

in contests, and she would win 1st prize. The painting

was her way of helping her escape all the madness that

she came from. At night she would stay up crying after

finding out that her mom gave her up at birth, and she

didn't know who her real dad was, but Lydia had a plan

on how she would fix everything. She wanted to put all

the missing pieces together one day.

Chapter 4

The Girls

Meanwhile, when Lydia is kidnapped and taken to an

underground warehouse in the western part of New

Mexico, the first night she is taken in, she cries the

whole night. Can you imagine spending time in a foster

home at the age of ten and then being kidnapped and

taken to a place where no one knows where you are?

This was Lydia's life in a nutshell. After the 3rd day of

being held underground, Lydia was drugged, but one of

the guys didn't drug her that much, and Lydia noticed

that the door wasn't locked in her room. The guy must

have forgotten to lock it. Lydia waits until the end of the

night and slightly opens the door, and runs toward the

back of the underground area. She notices that it leads

to some exit, but she is a little drugged, so she goes

back to her room with the memory of a way that she

may be able to get free one day. As she returns to her

room, she lays under the cover as if she had never left

her room. Every girl was being drugged every other

night, and some days they would be taken down to

Mexico and forced to sleep with guys for money on

street corners in the roughest parts of Mexico.

Meanwhile, detectives were still on their search, they were getting closer and closer as to where Lydia was being held, but they still just couldn't put their finger on where she was being kept. Somedays, the guys would let Lydia sit in the hallway with the other girls, and the girls would talk to each other. Each one would remember the other's phone numbers in case they'd ever get out of there. But one afternoon, Detective Hopkins received a call from another Detective located in the same town where Lydia was being held captive. The Detective says that one of the deputies ran a license plate check one morning after following the same van

Lydia was taking away in. Detective Hopkins reported to his police department that they should swarm that entire area until they found that van again. The Detective of that town didn't think to pull the van over, he just happened to run their plates, but nothing serious came up. Lydia's foster parents were nervous wrecks, and they would go to the police station at least once a week to get updates. So, it was a Saturday, and one of the girls tried to escape, but they caught her and dragged her to the hallway in front of all the other girls, and one of the guys shot her in front of the other girls. They wanted to make an example out of her to the rest of the girls so they would know the consequences of

trying to escape. These poor girls were traumatized

after seeing one of the girls get murdered in front of

their eyes. At that point, they had it in their mind that

there was no more hope for them.

Chapter 5

<u>Will I Survive</u>

Lydia slightly had an idea where she was, but not quite

precisely; day by day, she tried to shake off the effects

of being drugged. At this point, she's in fear of being a

part of the girls that get taken to a part where she is

forced to give sex in return for money. She wasn't even

with her foster parents for a year before something like

this happened. In the back of her mind, she wants to

know where the trail leads that are in the back of the

underground layer, they're being held in. Ever so often,

one of the guys leaves a razor blade sitting on the

counter inside Lydia's room, leaving her with the option

to commit suicide. Somedays, she thinks about it, but

deep down, she knows that if she did that, she wouldn't

be able to one day reunite with her birth parents, who

gave her up for adoption when she was a baby. The

search for Lydia is on, and detectives are doing

everything they can to find her; Somedays, Lydia stares

over at the blade on the counter next to the door,

contemplating if she should end it all. From being

adopted to being kidnapped, she's battling with

thoughts that tell her she's going to die there at the

hands of one of the kidnappers, and there are times when she folds her hands in the middle of the night to prays to God that someone comes and saves her. Every other day that goes by, heroin is injected into her veins. She doesn't know how much more she can take at this point. A window in her room is pinned shut, and the handles are flushed with caulking glue. Somedays, she stares off into the outside, wondering what it feels like to be free and what it feels like to be with family, biological family! The files she came across say that her real mom fled to Salt Lake City, Utah. The foster home would pull records to keep track of her. Everything about Lydia's mom was in the foster home database.

Lydia got a hold of those files and kept them in her bags

in her foster parent's home in the room closet. The guys

who kidnapped Lydia went back one morning and set

fire to the white van they had been driving, and they

felt like detectives were hot on their trail, so they had to

find a way to stay hidden. One of the guys was smoking

a cigarette on the rooftop of the warehouse. After he

finished smoking, he flicked the cigarette over the

rooftop onto the ground where they had set the van on

fire, there was still gas on the ground, and the lit

cigarette fell onto a gas line located near the building

immediately. There was an explosion on site. The kidnappers had to evacuate all seventeen girls, including Lydia, so that they wouldn't get burned, and they had to do it quickly so the police or fire department wouldn't notice what was going on underneath the warehouse. One of the kidnappers took a rope, tied all the girls together hand-by-hand, and loaded them into an old RV with San Diego, California License plates, which happens to be the state with the highest human trafficking cases in the country!

Chapter 6

<u>The Escape</u>

As the girls are tied together in the RV, one of the girls

begs and pleads that she needs to use the restroom

badly, not knowing that she intends to make a run for it

as soon as she gets outside. She couldn't use the RV

restroom because it was out of order considering the RV

was very old. One of the kidnappers suspected

something, but he just couldn't put his finger on what

she was trying to do. As she exits the RV, she pulls down

her pants and asks for privacy, and as soon as he walks

away, she hurries and runs at high speed! As she's

running, she falls and gets back up quickly while waving

her hand at passing cars, hoping to get help. All this

occurs in the western part of New Mexico, somewhere

near Tohatchi. The girl who got away is Amanda, and

she knows that she cannot get caught, so she runs

through a trail of woods. These woods lead to a nearby

town where she eventually can tell the first person, she

sees about what's going on. She happens to run into a

store crying and pleading for help. The store clerk asks,

"what's wrong? What's wrong" Amanda screams to the

top of her lungs and says, "sixteen other girls and I were

kidnapped, but I got away" Please help me, please help

me, as she pleads. The store clerk helps Amanda calm

down as they hurry to the back of the store so she can

get the full story of what's going on. As Amanda

describes everything, she starts from the beginning,

where she was first kidnapped. She was at a pool party

in a hotel near Arizona one afternoon during the

summer. As she was swimming and having a good time,

she suddenly had to use the restroom. When she came

out of the restroom, she heard a guy says, "hurry up

and grab her. Let's go" One of the guys had a small rag

covering Amanda's nose and mouth as she passed out

from the smell of chloroform on the rag. By the time

they took her away, she had no idea where she was

because she was blindfolded, just like every other girl

kidnapped. The store clerk wraps Amanda up with a big

blanket so she can sit and tell the rest of what has been

happening. The store manager warms her up with hot

cocoa to drink simply because it is freezing outside.

Meanwhile, the rest of the girls in the RV were still

miserable on the inside, wondering if they would ever

see their families again. They were out near the state

line between Colorado and New Mexico. They stayed in

the RV in an open field for the next couple of days until

they figured out where they would take the girls. Lydia

was tied to the rest of the girls, but near the back of the

RV, the drugs they gave her were just now starting to

wear off. Lydia wanted to make a run for it like Amanda,

but it was too late because, by now, the guys were

already alert for any more tricks. One of the girls even

thought about playing as far as getting away as Amanda

takes a few sips of her cocoa with two hands as her

whole-body quivers in fear and chill from the weather.

Chapter 7

<u>Sex Trafficking</u>

Despite all the psychological damage Amanda experienced in the kidnapping, she managed to break free from the traumatic situations plaguing her. After a few days in an open field on the side of the road, the girls were always on edge because they didn't know what to expect or what was going to happen next. Next, the girls were taken down to Tenancingo, Mexico, a city known for sex trafficking since the 1970s. The girls were tied to each other the entire trip, they hadn't eaten in days, and none of them had a bath. The girls weren't allowed to do anything out of the sight of any of the guys. By the time they made it to Tenancingo, there was a street that was filled with night clubs and inside these nightclubs, there wasn't any dancing going on, it was women and girls who had no choice but to solicit their bodies for money or they would have been beaten up badly or killed for not following orders. They ended up parking the RV on a back road where it was extremely dark without street lights. This was an old town known for dangerous incidents to happen. It was rumored that not even the police did their job in that town because they were afraid of cartel members. It was also said that the cartel would use women and kids they exploited by smuggling drugs to them to cross the border to expand their profits.

As all the girls were tied together in this RV, one of them had a nervous breakdown, and she couldn't take it anymore. What was going on drove her crazy, the men took most of the girls inside of these sex trafficking nightclubs on a strip in the town, But the girl who lost her mind was left inside of the RV, tied to the bed on the inside. Three different places had a pool table, a bar, and Tejano music playing. The men took all the girls and split them into three groups. On the inside of each one, they made a set of girls sit around at tables, and if men wanted sexual pleasures, they'd have to pay the girl one-hundred dollars for thirty minutes. There were empty rooms located in the back of each club, and each room had a bed. Before these girls were kidnapped, they lived normal lives with their families. They had no idea that they would end up as sex slaves while being drugged every other day, Detective Hopkins was called out to come to check out the location where the girls were last being held, but he was a bit too late when Hopkins searched the abandoned warehouse after it burned down, he found girl clothing lying on the floors of the building, along with drug needles scattered all over the place, and one of the girls who were murdered was left in one of the rooms of the warehouse, she was burnt to ashes lying in one of the empty rooms. But as the Detective searched the entire building cover to cover, he found a small purse wallet that one of the girls left behind. The wallet belonged to Amanda, the girl who escaped from the RV. When detectives searched her name, they discovered she was twenty-one years old. Detective Hopkins visited Amanda's parents that week to ask questions concerning Amanda's whereabouts. But the following day, Detective received a call saying that Amanda was in a store near Farmington, New Mexico, where she ran away after escaping. Meanwhile, at one of the spots where the girls were located, one guy was extremely drunk and high and became overly aggressive with one of the girls. When the club owner discovered this, he told one of the guys who brought the girls there. He immediately rushed to the RV to grab his gun and came back to shoot the guy in the head direct range. The girl screamed at the top of her lungs, but there was nobody there to hear or help her. She ran out of the club with half her clothes on, trying to get help, and one of the guys ran and grabbed her to drag her back to the RV

until the night ended.

Chapter 8

The Client

Lisa, the girl who shared a room with Lydia at the foster home she stayed at, became a dancer at a strip club in Sante Fe. Some nights, Lisa would do coke in the women's restroom at the club, it would give her an edge to want to dance more, and it made her not so shy. The guys would buy her all types of drinks throughout the night, but she would catch an Uber back and forth so she wouldn't have to drive drunk behind the wheel. One night at the club on a Saturday, Lisa met a guy who soon became a client. She normally wouldn't do anything besides dance, Until the night she met Kevin! Kevin was a high roller, and he drove a black

Bentley with crème leather seats on the inside; he showed it to her on his phone while she was sitting in his lap. Then he told her that he had a connection on coke, and that pretty much sealed the deal between the two; he lived about thirty minutes away in a three-story condo downtown, he asked if she wanted to stay the night, and he'll take her home the next morning, but she was like no I don't go home with the men here I dance. But he made an offer she couldn't refuse. He said if you stay with me one night, I'll pay you a thousand dollars cash, Lisa saw what type of lifestyle he lived and said I guess with just this one guy wouldn't hurt. She said to wait for me outside while I ran to the dressing room to change and grab my things. She met him outside, and they got in the car and drove off! On the way to his place, she asked him what he does for a living. He looked over at her and said, "If I tell you, I'd have to kill you." She gave him a nervous look, then he busted out laughing and said seriously, I own a few car washes, and I'm heavy into real estate. She says what type of real estate? He says I own 100 homes, and I lease half of them through a Hud housing program, and he makes a joke, "so my money comes on time like a stopwatch" Kevin had a bit of a sense of humor, and Lisa tends to like that, but she still felt butterflies in her stomach because she had never gone home with anyone from the club before. As they slowly pull up to his place, he parks his car, and they leave to go inside. As soon as she is in, she looks down and sees that his entire living room floor is made of aquarium glass, and there are all kinds of fish swimming underneath. Lisa was impressed by the sight of it all! He is her what type of wine she prefers, and she says in a shy tone, "Merlo," one glass of Merlo comes up. Kevin says. He puts on some soft R&B and tells her to get comfortable. She looks over and says I'd like to take a nice bath if you don't mind, He says sure, you don't mind if I join you, do you? she says that's fine with me! As she walks into the bathroom and flicks the light, she sees a stand-up shower and whirlpool tub; both are made of Gold! Lisa got tired of holding back the question she had wanted to ask since she first got in his car. After a few glasses of wine, she asks, how come you don't have a wife? He says to run the bath water, and I'll explain after we get in. As they sit in the water, she sits in his lap, and he explains his past relationship. He says I used to be married 6 years ago, but one day he got halfway to work and completely left his briefcase in the closet, so he drove back home and noticed a car he had never seen before parked across the street from his house, he thought that was strange but paid it no attention. He pulled out his house keys to unlock the door, but it happened to be unlocked. He figured she'd forgotten to lock the door after he left earlier, but she normally never forgets to lock the door when he leaves for work every morning. When he walked in, he got halfway down the hall to see his room door closed. Something told him to put his ear to the door after seeing the strange car parked across the street outside. When he puts his ear to the door, he immediately hears his wife moaning loudly! When he opened the door out of rage, his wife of ten years was in bed with another man, His heart sank to his stomach, and before he thought about making any irrational decisions, he decided just to leave, and that day, he left everything behind and moved on with his life. A year later, what his wife did to him turned him into a savage when it came to women. For an entire two years, Kevin slept with over two hundred and fifty women after leaving nightclubs. After Kevin explains what happened to him and his ex-wife, he picks Lisa up out of the tub, dries her off, and then takes her to the room, and they both have illicit sex for at least an hour! They wake up the next morning, and Kevin pays Lisa her thousand dollars and tells her there's more ccc[Where that came from... So, weeks on average, they continued meeting up and sleeping together, And the more they met up, the more money he gave her. Within a month, she made ten thousand dollars from sleeping with Kevin, but one weekend she said that this would be her last draw; it was the last night of them together. After the first few times, they stopped using condoms. That night, Kevin was so drunk that he slept in the living room on the couch after they had sex. The next morning, Lisa got up to go grab her heels from Kevin's closet, but curiosity began to strike. As she begins to look through his closet, she sees a bottle of prescription meds. Something told her to read the label, and she saw Kevin's name and below it was the dosages, but to the right, she saw three large letters on the bold print that said H.I.V She immediately dropped the bottle and put her clothes on in a rage of panic and stormed out of his house crying out of fear of being infected. A week later, she tested positive and found out she had aids, that same week, Lisa was in her restroom at home. She drank an entire bottle of bleach to the head, passed out on her bathroom floor, and died.

Chapter 9

Connecting The Dots

Detective Hopkins finds himself back in front of his bulletin board at home that had Lydia's picture tact to it. As he begins to make him a hot cup of coffee, He starts the coffee maker. Once it gets done, he pours his coffee with a few teaspoons of sugar and cream as he literally sits in front of the bulletin board with a few missing persons on it. Almost a year has passed, and Detective thought long and hard about closing Lydia's file. There was no sign of her anywhere, no leads or anything. Hopkins fell asleep in front of the bulletin board, hoping he could put things all in perspective. Lydia happened to be the youngest missing person on his bulletin board, and he sat in front of the bulletin for hours and hours, trying to come up with any lead he could find. That same day he went out to the office to have a talk with his partner, the other Detective. The two-start looking heavily into numerous other human trafficking cases throughout that entire region. They noticed that he was a pattern of how girls were being abducted, and they ended up matching these incidents with the same group of men being taken in for custody but never held long enough in jail. The detectives started putting two and two together and began to pull the files of these same gentlemen, getting their addresses to go out and speak to them. As I said early on, there was a pattern in these men, and that pattern was that the girls were always in a public place with one or two parents. One guy was always taking the pictures, while the other was the kidnapper. They worked together as a team. The two detectives notice a lead that may send them in the direction they need to go. One of those same guys had a place they would always be from time to time, and that place was the guy's aunt, who usually knew about what the guys were Into, but she withheld a lot of information to protect her nephew from going back to jail, but this time her nephew wasn't willing to go back to jail because he knew he wouldn't get off so easy the next time. At his aunt's house, he would keep things in the attic, like tons of unmarked cash and other things like weapons and things of that nature, and he would always find himself going back to visit his aunt, so he could have access to the cash and weapons if he needed. So, Detective Hopkins sent a steak out of the unit to watch the aunt's house in case they'd see the guy when he was there. Detective Hopkins was back tied into this case heavily with his partner, but Hopkins would put more time into Lydia's case than any other case. It was something about her case that made him focus more on it than anyone else's. They knew that wherever Lydia was being held, she had to still be within range of Sante Fe. Something deep down told him that, especially since a white van was pulled over in another part of the same town. With Hopkins finding out about one of the guy aunts, he just knew it wouldn't be long before he'd crack this case. It had been at least a year and some months since she'd been kidnapped.

Chapter 10

<u>Escaping The Trauma</u>

At this point, Lydia had no idea that her old friend Lisa committed suicide just days ago. The girls were still being held down in Mexico. Some days they were taken down certain streets in bad areas to solicit themselves at night and in the mornings. Lydia was the youngest out of all the girls, and she was scared for her life every single moment. Days upon days, not knowing if she would survive from drug intake. One night they made Lydia dress up in skimpy clothing and took her out on one of the tracks to make money. Fifteen-year-old Lydia was whistled to one of the cars on the strip. It was an older-looking white guy that drove a blue Iroc-Z

Camaro; as Lydia gets on the passenger side, her stomach is in a rage with nervousness at the fact that she's being forced to commit an adult act at her age. As the guy driving decides to make the block, He tries to place his hand on Lydia's lap, but she isn't going for it. She slaps the guy and quickly jumps out of the car while it's moving slowly. As she jumped out of the moving car, she ran as fast as she could to the first place she saw, but everything was closed. One of her kidnappers ends up snatching her up and bringing her back to where the other girls are being held. All the girls were taken to a hideaway spot in an open field in the slums of Mexico. When Lydia gets escorted back into the RV, over half the girls are crying because one of the other guys had a huge knife to one of the girl's throats as he yells out,

"YOU DO AS I SAY OR YOU WILL DIE" When Lydia saw this, she was frightened to death at what she was witnessing that girl go through. Things started to die down that night as it became closer to the time to sleep. Some of the older girls slept on the floor and let Lydia sleep on the bed in the RV, slightly because she was the youngest of them all and because they felt she needed a good night's rest because of what she went through earlier the night. That night, the guy who threatened the girl on the RV with the knife attempted to rape that girl in the back of the RV. As he began to force himself on her, she started screaming for her life at the top of her lungs. At this point, the rest of the girls had enough, and they wanted to protect the girl from being raped, so one of the girls took the knife from the guy while he was sleeping earlier, and they all piled on top of the guy one by one and drags him off the girl, they began beating him up bad, at this time Lydia is sound asleep. The other guys had gone out clubbing looking for a new girl to kidnap, so this was a perfect time for the girls to escape it, they all held the guy down on the floor, and one of the girls took the knife and shoved it deep into his side as he slowly bleeds out to die! The girls take the keys to the RV out of his pockets as he lies there to die, All the girls are in a state of shock, and their adrenaline is pumping from killing the guy! One of the older girls named Nancy takes the keys, starts the RV, and hits the road, it is about 3 am, and they drive straight to the nearest police station

Chapter 11

<u>A Visit from The Local Detective</u>

Before you knew it, Posters of Lydia were all over Santa Fe, New Mexico, and Detective Hopkins decided to pay the aunt of one of the kidnappers a visit. The Detective knew that this was a dangerous move considering that these men were also tied in with the Cartel, but this was his line of work and what he signed up for. As he walks up to knock on the door, The aunt, in a loud voice, says, "who is it?" Detective Hopkins says! When she opens the door, he asks if it's ok if he comes in to have a talk with her briefly. She agrees for him to come in. He sits on the couch and explains why he's there. Sophia was her name. She politely asks him what brings him to my home detective, and he explains that your nephew and a few other men may have been tied to a possible kidnapping a year ago. He asks Sophia if she has noticed any strange activity from her nephew within the past year or so. She nods, grabs her chest, and says not that I know of. He sometimes goes into the attic to set some traps for the rats when he comes here. Detective Hopkins asks Sophia, Mam do you mind if I come back another time with my partner to check out some things in your attic? It's strictly police business, that's all! Sophia agrees and says sure, and I don't mind one bit. Sophia begins to whisper in a low tone to ask the Detective, is my Danny in trouble? Detective says at this moment, no, but if our evidence ties him to this missing girl's case, he could be doing a lot of time! The Detective explains to Sophia that more girls are involved in this kidnapping, and we want to find the underlying cause of this. Sophia is nervous as her hands begin to shake. She asks the Detective, is that all for today, sir? Hopkins says yes, mam, but my partner and I will be back in a few days to check out that attic! She walks him to the front door as he exits. As he walks to his car, he hears loud gunshots from the next street over, and the aunt lives in a perilous neighborhood. As soon as Detective left, Sophia ed her nephew's cell phone to ask him if there was something that she wanted to tell me, Danny boy. He says in a nervous tone, no, auntie, why is that she says, just asking Danny because if there were, you would tell me, right? Yes, Auntie, of course, she knew by the sound of his voice that he was hiding something, so she decided not to tell Danny about the Detective that

stopped by her home.

Chapter 12

<u>The Interrogation</u>

Detective Brown and Detective Hopkins worked on the case of Lisa and her suicide. They later did an autopsy on Lisa and discovered that all the drinks she had with Kevin when they were at his home were laced with powdered substances. Brown and Hopkins decided to look deeper into this case since she was an old friend of Lydia; they figured they could find a missing link to Lydia's case if they dug a bit deeper! With all evidence leading back to Kevin in the case of Lisa's suicide, a unit was sent out to take Kevin in for questioning. After they pick him up, he sits in the Lobby handcuffed and asks one of the detectives to get him a pack of cigarettes before their interrogation begins. Detective Brown noticed that Kevin was sweating a bit drastically in the Lobby. As questioning began, Hopkins placed his glasses on the table and continued his coffee-drinking routine when dealing with this case. Hopkins began to just stare at Kevin as if he almost knew he was hiding something more than just drugging Lisa. Brown Leans over the table, looks Kevin in the eyes, and says, "Tell me what you know." Hopkins takes a break from sipping his coffee and says, "I think He already knows we know" the detectives were using an investigation tactic on Kevin, pretending as if they knew something already, A tactic that made criminals sweat even more. They immediately gave in at the sight of the stare from Brown and Hopkins after their tactic. Kevin remained quiet as he sat smoking his cigarette down to the butt.

Once they got on the topic of Lisa, Kevin took his last

cigarette hit and asked both detectives, so how much

time are they trying to give me? Hopkins says what do

you mean time? We haven't even discussed a crime yet.

Hopkins again looked deep into Kevin's eyes and said,

I'm a ask you again, "to tell me everything that

happened from the beginning."

Chapter 13

Putting The Missing Pieces Together

Steven and Michelle, Lydia's foster parents, had gone
to different parts of New Mexico to hang posters of
Lydia's picture, and they were doing all they could to do
their part to help detectives find their daughter. They
were trying not to let time convince them that they
would never find her. The detectives always kept both
parents in good high positive spirits and helped them
understand that they should not give up. Detective
Hopkins ended up investigating the small purse that
belonged to one of the girls at the location that burnt to
the ground. Hopkins found out that there was an
address of the girl's parents in her purse, so Detective

Brown and Hopkins set a date to go out and speak to the girl's parents. Shortly afterward, the detectives had gotten a phone call from a Detective who worked for a police department in the part of Mexico where the girls were taken the night, they were forced to solicit in one of the clubs, Detective Vasquez worked for Tenancingo police station and overheard the story of a missing girl in New Mexico, and after someone heard the gunshots at the club the night one of the girls were dragged out by her hair. There was an older Spanish Lady that was closing her place of business one night and saw the men and the missing girls walking back to their RV that night. The older lady knew something wasn't right because the girls were dressed half-naked and walking with the two men. She thought to herself, with that area being known for human trafficking, she figured that's what

was going on, so she decided to call the nearest police

station to talk to Detective Vasquez; she even grabbed

her cell phone and took pictures of all the girls walking

together, she said they all looked so exhausted to the

point where they were walking with their hills in hand

walking barefooted from being on their feet

consistently.

Chapter 14

Being Rescued

One of the guys that were stabbed to death by one of

the girls allowed the girls to make a smooth getaway to

seek help. They ended up driving the RV to the nearest

police station; on their way to the station, they

suddenly got a flat tire and were forced to pull to the

side of the road. They were about 2 miles away from

the police station in Southeast Mexico in San Pablo Del

Monte, and they had to sleep in the RV until morning

the next day eventually. The girls were so relieved that

they didn't know how to react. The following day they

were all practically covered in blankets because it was cold outside. The girls happened to be in Luck because a police officer was driving past, and he decided to check out of the RV, where he saw that there was a flat tire; as he got out of his car and approached the RV, he stepped back to hold his gun on his waist because one of the girls came out of the RV running and crying full speed towards the officer, he yells out "what's wrong what's wrong." She screams at the top of her lungs, "help us, please"!!!!! The officer steps inside the RV and walks to the back as he smells a weird smell. He notices the dead body of one of the guys the girls stabbed lying toward the back of the RV. The officer asks the girls in a mild

tone, why is there a dead body in this RV, and what's

going on? The officer sees that Lydia is the youngest of

all the girls, but he still can't quite figure out what is

going on. One of the girls, Nancy, said they were all

kidnapped almost a year ago. The officer transports

them to the nearest station, where they each get to tell

their story one by one! Steven and Michelle had no idea

their daughter was in police custody in Mexico. They

had been patiently waiting on a response from

detectives about an update. When detectives got the

call, they were shocked and couldn't wait to tell Lydia's

parents.

Chapter 15

<u>Case Solved</u>

Lydia and the rest of the girls were escorted back to the

Santa Fe, New Mexico, police station where Detective

Brown and Detective Hopkins are stationed. Steven and

Michelle raced up to the police station when they heard

the news; when they got to the front doors of the police

station, they felt nervous because the last time they saw

Lydia was a year ago. Every parent of each girl was

called. The police station was jammed packed with

news reporters, and the girls were wrapped in blankets

with sobs of tears crying as their parents showed up one

by one. On November 27th, 2007, the case of Lydia

Sanchez was solved!

Made in the USA
Middletown, DE
08 June 2023

31905310R00042